Author Day for Room 3T

by Robin Pulver · illustrated by Chuck Richards

CLARION BOOKS / NEW YORK

Clarion Books
a Houghton Mifflin Company imprint
215 Park Avenue South, New York, NY 10003
Text copyright © 2005 by Robin Pulver
Illustrations copyright © 2005 by Chuck Richards

The illustrations were executed in watercolor and colored pencil.
The text was set in 16-point Hadriano Light.

www.houghtonmifflinbooks.com

Manufactured in China

Library of Congress Cataloging-in-Publication Data

Pulver, Robin.
Author day for room 3T / by Robin Pulver ; illustrated by Chuck Richards.
p. cm.
Summary: Mr. Topple's third-grade class prepares for the arrival of author
Harry Bookman, with unexpected results.
ISBN 0-618-35406-9
[Authors—Fiction. Books and reading—Fiction. Schools—Fiction.]
I. Richards, Chuck, 1957– ill. II. Title
PZ7.P97325 Au 2005
[E]—dc22
2004014719

ISBN-13: 978-0-618-35406-1
ISBN-10: 0-618-35406-9

SCP 10 9 8 7 6 5 4 3 2 1

To the extraordinary children's book authors in my two critique groups: Tedd Arnold, Mary Jane Auch, Patience Brewster, Bruce Coville, Cynthia DeFelice, Alice DeLaCroix, Marsha Hayles, Jennifer Meagher, Vivian Vande Velde, and Ellen Stoll Walsh. May all your visits be happy ones!
— R. P.

To my daughter, Kim, who patiently served as my model for most of the characters in this book (excluding, of course, "Harry Bookman")
— C. R.

It was Reading Week at Lerner Elementary School. The students in Room 3T, Mr. Topple's third-grade class, were expecting a special guest. Harry Bookman, a real live author, was coming for a visit at the end of the week.

Harry Bookman had written some of the silliest books in the school library. Books like *The Mystery of the Missing Monkey Bars* and *Ants in My Lunch Box* and *The Banana from Outer Space*.

To get ready for their visitor, 3T read Harry Bookman's books forward. They read his books backward. They read his books upside down. They drew pictures to illustrate his stories and hung them on the walls. They made up songs about his stories and sang them in music class.

They dressed up as his characters and acted out his stories for the kindergartners. They painted a big welcome banner and hung it up in the library.

"Do you think Harry Bookman will arrive in a rocket ship, like the one in *The Banana from Outer Space*?" Dexter asked the librarian, Mrs. Storey.

"No, he plans to come by car," said Mrs. Storey. "Believe it or not, authors are ordinary people, like you and me."

The children in Mr. Topple's class didn't believe it. If authors were ordinary, why all the fuss and bother about this one?

Mr. Topple seemed even more excited than the kids. He told his students to write down questions to ask Harry Bookman. "Serious questions, about writing and being an author," he insisted. "No monkey business."

So the children wrote questions like:

"Do you write your stories by hand or type them on the computer?"

"Do you like writing for children?"

"Where do you get your ideas?"

But at the drinking fountain, Dexter and Skippy wondered, "Do authors get thirsty? What do they eat? Is Harry Bookman rich?"

And on the playground, Trixie and Esmerelda wondered, "What kind of car does Harry Bookman drive? What does he look like? Do authors like to have fun?"

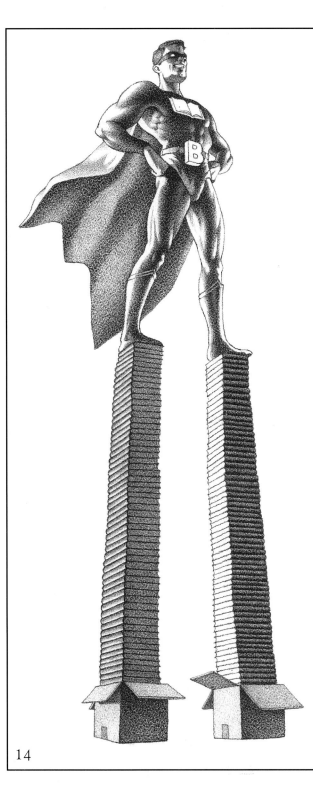

Finally, it was the last day of Reading Week—Author Day for Room 3T! Mr. Topple sent Trixie and Dexter to the library to find out if Harry Bookman had arrived. "If you see someone there who looks new and different," he told them, "you can be sure it's the author."

Trixie and Dexter hurried to the library. There was no sign of the librarian. No sign of anyone. But then . . . *rap . . . tap . . . tap!* A noise at the window. A grinning face.

"New and different!" exclaimed Dexter. He opened the window, and in hopped the visiting author.

"Wait right here," said Trixie. "We'll go get the rest of the class."

On their way back to Room 3T, Trixie and Dexter met Mrs. Storey in the hall. "Harry Bookman is here!" they told her.

"Oh, dear," said Mrs. Storey. "I'm in such a tizzy over this visit, I almost forgot ice water for the author. On top of that, I seem to have misplaced my glasses."

Trixie and Dexter steered her toward the library. Then they went to their classroom.

"Harry Bookman is here!" they said to Mr. Topple.

"You'll see why his name is Harry," they whispered to their classmates.

"Go on ahead to the library, children," said Mr. Topple. "I'm going to gather up your drawings to show to Mr. Bookman. Then I'll join you."

18

When the students filed into the library, the visiting author was standing on the librarian's desk, inspecting the microphone. He grinned at the children as they sat down on the carpet, and they grinned back.

Mrs. Storey peered around the room. "Students?" she said. "I can't see much without my glasses, so please be on your best behavior and welcome Harry Bookman."

"Good morning, Mr. Bookman," the children said together.

The author jumped up and down. He scooped ice cubes out of his water and tossed them everywhere. He panted and hooted in a raspy voice.

"Oh, dear," said the librarian. "Apparently, Harry Bookman has laryngitis, so he can't give his speech. But perhaps he can still answer your questions."

Suddenly, loud noises came from the hallway. *Ka-boom! Clatter! Crash! Clankety-clank!*

The children jumped. The author screamed. Mrs. Storey felt her way to the library door and closed it. "Sorry about the ruckus— whatever it was," she said. "Now, go ahead, children. Ask your questions."

The students learned a lot about the visiting author. When they asked which of his books he liked the best, he scratched his head. Then he picked up a copy of *The Banana from Outer Space* and gave it a big smooch.

When they asked who his favorite author was, he tapped his chest, clapped his hands, and grinned.

And when they asked if he liked writing for children, he hopped down from the desk and gave hugs all around.

At the reception in the gym, the visiting author batted the balloons. He gobbled banana bread and fruit salad and slurped orange punch. When he spied the climbing rope dangling from the ceiling, he scrambled up and swung back and forth, back and forth, hooting happily.

"No wonder he writes children's books," said Dexter. "Harry Bookman is a kid at heart!"

23

Back in the library, the author autographed copies of his books and tossed them to the students. They turned the books every which way, trying to read the signature. "Harry Bookman must type his stories on the computer," said Esmerelda. "He is *not* a neat writer."

Suddenly, a red-faced woman burst into the room. "There you are!" she exclaimed, grabbing the visiting author by the hand. Then she turned to Mrs. Storey and the children. "We were on our way to the television studio for a guest appearance," she said. "But when I stopped for gas, this rascal slipped out of the van. I've been looking for him for hours."

"Wow!" said Skippy. "We didn't know he was a TV star, too!"

"We really enjoyed his visit," said Trixie.

"Well, it's no surprise he found his way here. He loves children," said the woman. "Thanks for making him feel welcome."

The kids from Room 3T walked the visiting author to the front door. They watched as the woman opened the passenger door of a big van and helped him inside. Then she got into the driver's seat and drove off.

"Harry Bookman must be rich," said Dexter. "He has his own driver for that van."

Just then Mr. Topple showed up. He was bandaged and limping.

"Mr. Topple! What happened? Where have you been?" his students asked.

"In the nurse's office," he replied. "I slipped on an ice cube in the hallway and crashed into the custodian's cart. I'm okay, but I'm sorry I didn't get to meet Harry Bookman."

A very ordinary looking man hurried up to the door, puffing and panting. "Visiting author," he huffed. "Got lost. Traffic jam! Detour! Terribly late. Harry Bookman!"

"Sorry," said Skippy. "He just left."

"Too bad you missed him," said Trixie, "because now we understand what all the fuss and bother was about."

"Yes," said Esmerelda. "Authors are *not* ordinary people like you and me."

Harry Bookman's Tips for Hosting a Successful Author Visit

Six weeks before the visit . . .
- Ask the author to send autobiographical information—along with a recent photograph. Or check the author's website.
- Begin reading the author's books. Read as many as possible.
- Choose which books you want the author to autograph and place your order with the publisher or supplier.

Two weeks before the visit . . .
- Send the author detailed directions to your school, indicating where to park and which entrance to use. Include the school's phone number in case the author gets lost.
- Let the author know which books the class has read.
- Find out what the author likes to eat for lunch or snack.
- Prepare a list of questions for the author.
- Contact your local newspaper. The editor may want to send a reporter and/or photographer to cover the visit.

On the day of the visit . . .
- Provide the author with drinking water, a microphone, and any special equipment he or she requests.
- Schedule plenty of time for the author to autograph books.

After the visit . . .
- Send a thank-you note, letters, pictures, or photos to show the author how much your class enjoyed the visit.

Have fun!